**Dear Parents,**

Welcome to the Scholastic Reader series. We have taken over 80 years of experience with teachers, parents, and children and put it into a program that is designed to match your child's interests and skills.

**Level 1**—Short sentences and stories made up of words kids can sound out using their phonics skills and words that are important to remember.

**Level 2**—Longer sentences and stories with words kids need to know and new "big" words that they will want to know.

**Level 3**—From sentences to paragraphs to longer stories, these books have large "chunks" of text and are made up of a rich vocabulary.

**Level 4**—First chapter books with more words and fewer pictures.

It is important that children learn to read well enough to succeed in school and beyond. Here are ideas for reading this book with your child:

- Look at the book together. Encourage your child to read the title and make a prediction about the story.
- Read the book together. Encourage your child to sound out words when appropriate. When your child struggles, you can help by providing the word.
- Encourage your child to retell the story. This is a great way to check for comprehension.

Scholastic Readers are designed to support your child's efforts to learn how to read at every age and every stage. Enjoy helping your child learn to read and love to read.

> **—Francie Alexander**
> Chief Education Officer
> Scholastic Education

Ms. Frizzle

Liz

Written by Anne Capeci
Illustrated by Carolyn Bracken

Sincere appreciation to Jonathan D.W. Kahl, Professor of Atmospheric
Science at the University of Wisconsin-Milwaukee, for his advice in the
preparation of the manuscript and illustrations.
Based on *The Magic School Bus* books
written by Joanna Cole and illustrated by Bruce Degen.

0-439-80108-7

40  39  38  37  36  35  34  33                                        16  17  18  19/0

Designed by Rick DeMonico.

Printed in the U.S.A. 40 First printing, April 2006

# The Magic School Bus®
## Rides the Wind

Arnold   Ralphie   Keesha   Phoebe   Carlos   Tim   Wanda   Dorothy Ann

SCHOLASTIC INC.

New York   Toronto   London   Auckland   Sydney
Mexico City   New Delhi   Hong Kong   Buenos Aires

1. How does the wind spread seeds?
2. What do weather balloons do?
3. How does a windmill work?
I'M GIVING MY KITE TO MY GRANDMA. IT'S HER BIRTHDAY.

We are on the ground.
The kite is in the sky.
How can we get it back?

Ms. Frizzle gets a twinkle in her eye.
"I know how," she says.
"Let's get on the bus!"

We get into the Magic School Bus.
The bus starts to change.
It becomes a hang glider.
Ms. Frizzle says it will catch the wind
just like a kite.

We are not the only ones flying on the wind.

**WIND MAKES THINGS GO**
by Phoebe

When wind pushes on things, it makes them go up.

KITE

HANG GLIDER

It makes them go forward.

SAILBOAT

And round and round, too.

WINDMILL

The bus changes again. Now it is
the Magic Weather Balloon!
We float up. And up.
Soon we are on top of the storm.
"I see clear skies!" Ms. Frizzle says.

WIND BLOWS BAD
WEATHER IN...

... AND OUT.

BUT WHERE DID
THE WIND BLOW
MY KITE?

UP, UP, AND AWAY!

ALL ABOUT
WEATHER BALLOONS
by Ralphie

Weather balloons can go 20 miles high. They have tools that tell us what the weather is like way up in the sky.

I WISH WE COULD CATCH WANDA'S KITE.
THE WIND SPREADS SEEDS
by Arnold
The wind helps new plants and trees grow.
The wind blows seeds far and wide. When the seeds land, they sprout into new plants.
MAPLE
DANDELION

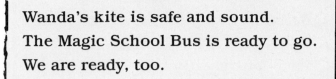

Wanda's kite is safe and sound.
The Magic School Bus is ready to go.
We are ready, too.

# HOW WE MEASURE WIND

We use special tools to measure wind:
An anemometer measures the speed of wind.

A wind sock shows how strong the wind is.
It shows which way the wind is going, too.